Ladybird  Readers

Tom's Birthday

To access the audio and digital versions
of this book:

1 Go to **www.ladybirdeducation.co.uk**
2 Click "Unlock book"
3 Enter the code below

AXQixYjFcP

Notes to teachers, parents, and carers

The **Ladybird Readers** Beginner level helps young language learners to become familiar with key conversational phrases in English. The language introduced has clear real-life applications, giving children the tools to hold their first conversations in English.

This book focuses on asking and responding to the question "Is this Tom's house?" and provides practice of saying "yes" and "no" in English. The pictures that accompany the text show street and party settings, which may be used to introduce one or two pieces of topic-based vocabulary, such as "party" and "gift", if the children are ready.

There are some activities to do in this book. They will help children practice these skills:

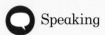 Speaking  Listening* Reading Singing*

*To complete these activities, listen to the audio downloads available at www.ladybirdeducation.co.uk

Series Editor: Sorrel Pitts
Text adapted by Nicole Irving
Song lyrics by Wardour Studios

LADYBIRD BOOKS

UK | USA | Canada | Ireland | Australia
India | New Zealand | South Africa

Ladybird Books is part of the Penguin Random House group of companies
whose addresses can be found at global.penguinrandomhouse.com.
www.penguin.co.uk   www.puffin.co.uk   www.ladybird.co.uk

Penguin
Random House
UK

Text adapted from *What If . . .?* by Anthony Browne, first published by Doubleday, 2013
This Ladybird Readers edition published 2021
001

Printed in China
A CIP catalogue record for this book is available from the British Library

ISBN: 978–0–241–47557–7

All correspondence to:
Ladybird Books
Penguin Random House Children's
One Embassy Gardens, 8 Viaduct Gardens, London SW11 7BW

FSC
www.fsc.org
MIX
Paper from
responsible sources
FSC® C018179

Ladybird Readers

Tom's Birthday

Based on *What If . . .?*
by Anthony Browne

"It is Tom's birthday,"
Mum says.

"Where is Tom's house?"
Joe says.

"Is this Tom's house?"
Joe says.

"No, Joe," Mum says.

"Is this Tom's house?"
Joe says.

8

"No, Joe," Mum says.

"Is this Tom's house?"
Joe says.
"Yes, Joe!" Mum says.

"Hello, Joe!" Tom says.
"Happy birthday, Tom!"
Joe says.

1 **Talk with a friend.** 💬

Is this Tom's house?

No.

Is this Tom's house?

Yes.

Hello, Tom!

2 Listen. Color in the words. 🎧 📖

1   yes   no

2   Tom   Joe

3   house   birthday

4   hello   happy birthday

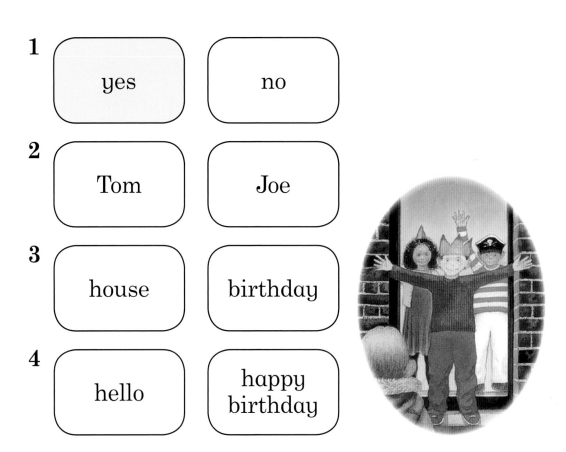

3 Sing the song.

It is Tom's birthday.
"Where is Tom's house?" says Joe.
Let's go to Tom's house! Here we go!

Happy, happy, happy birthday!
Happy birthday, Tom!
Hello, Tom! Hello, Joe! Happy birthday!

"Is this Tom's house?" Joe says.
"No, Joe," Mum says.
"Is this Tom's house?" Joe says.
"Yes, Joe!" Mum says.